Hostile Hearts

The Collector Series Book 1 - A Deadly Obsession

C. C. Sleeth

CONTENTS

CHAPTER ONE

THE MATCH

SHE'S NOT BEAUTIFUL NOW.

Not with the blood seeping between her teeth, not with the red ribbon biting into her throat, not with her nails broken to the quick from scratching at the restraints.

But she's **perfect**.

"Almost done, Lily."

My voice is soft. Gentle. Like a lover's promise.

She whimpers. Not words anymore. Just the wet, ragged sound of a throat worn raw from screaming.

I drag the blade—deliberate, slow—along the curve of her hip. Just deep enough to make her flinch. Just shallow enough not to end it yet. I want her to **feel** this. Every inch of it. Better yet, I want her to feel every inch of me as I part her legs, revealing the glistening proof of the pleasure I gave her—still lingering, even now, despite the restraints.

She's always loved the game— but this isn't the bedroom fantasy she used to whisper about in the dark. This is silence soaked in sweat and dread. This is a surrender carved into skin.

She doesn't know it yet. Not fully. But her body remembers. She's still slick. Still open. Still begging without breath.

I kneel between her thighs like a worshipper at a ruined altar. My mouth finds the rim of her ass, and I drag my tongue along the edge— slow. reverent. She tries to flinch, but the restraints hold. They always do.

Her moan is strangled beneath the gag. It's not fear. Not exactly. It's the sound of a woman unraveling— torn between the truth and the lie she used to tell herself: that pain like this can be played with.

God, I want to ruin her with it. I want to make her disappear inside the ache. I want to fuck her ghost.

And I'm so hard it hurts.

I drag my tongue slowly—possessively—through her folds, tasting the wet heat that still clings to her like a secret. She arches, helpless in her restraints, back bowed in offering. I tease her, circling, dipping, savoring. Not for her pleasure. For mine.

Then I find her clit. Flick. Flick. The way she likes. The way she whispered for me to do it, those first few nights when she still thought this was love.

"I've never had anyone make me squirm the way you do," she told me once, as she tried to pull away, almost falling off the bed, as I pulled her back underneath me.

Oh, Lily ... if only you knew what those words did to me. The pleasure you give me when you say them. The way I'm going to make you feel in the end—

You've belonged to me since the moment I found you again.

"You always wanted to be seen," I murmur. "All those photos. All those lies. Look at you now. Raw. Honest. Finally real."

Her breathing turns jagged, shallow—close. She's going to come fast this time. I can feel it in the way her thighs tense, in the way her body opens beneath the bind.

She loves this— The restraints. The helplessness. The power stolen and given back in gasps.

She told me once that this was her favorite game. And tonight, I'm not holding back.

I drive three fingers deep into her ass, while my other hand works her clit in tight, practiced circles.

She writhes—trapped and trembling—until she breaks, screaming through the gag as her climax tears through her like a storm.

Her pulse flutters beneath the ribbon—fragile, beautiful. This is the moment. The moment I collect her. The moment she becomes mine—fully, eternally.

And in this breath, right before the end, I think about the beginning.

Her laugh. High school cafeteria. Sophomore year. My tray hit the floor. Spaghetti splattered across my boots. And Lily Grant's laugh cut through me sharper than any blade I've ever held.

"Poodle Boy! Look at those curls!"

Her friends joined in. But it was her voice—light, cruel, unforgettable—that buried itself under my skin.

That moment never left me. And now, neither will she.

Her final breath shudders against the ribbon. A soft, pitiful thing.

Perfect.

My hand tightens. The blade gleams.

"Time to smile for me, Lily."

Her eyes—bloodshot, wide, glossy with terror—lock on mine. I wait. There's always something at the end. A final twitch of rebellion. A lie. A plea.

But Lily? She does something else. She laughs. A broken, gurgling thing. Half-spit. Half-madness. All Lily.

"F-fuck you," she rasps.

Her voice is shredded, but the words land sharp. Defiant. Even now, she has claws. Good. It means there's still something to take.

"I knew," she chokes. "I knew you were a freak back then. Should've drowned you in that spaghetti."

I lean in, nose brushing the edge of her cheekbone. Her blood smells like copper and dust.

"Should've," I whisper. "But you didn't. You laughed instead. And that laugh made you mine."

Her breath rattles. Short. Panicked. I slide the blade beneath the ribbon, not to cut her free, but to trace the edge where silk meets skin. Her pulse flickers beneath it.

"I've been waiting to hear you laugh again," I murmur. "And now that I have... we can end this."

I press. Just enough. Her lips part. But this time, she doesn't laugh. She sobs.

And then—

FLASH.

One Month Earlier

Lily: "Hey, you look familiar … same gym maybe? "

Her message pops up like a casual slap in the face.

We matched five minutes ago.

I hadn't even opened her full profile yet—hadn't decided what version of myself I'd feed her—and already she's in my inbox.

> ***Lily:*** *"Hey, you look familiar ... same gym maybe?"*

Cute. I tap her photo and let the full façade unravel.

The dating app is one of the cleaner ones. A little classier than the hookup trash. That's her speed—still wants to seem wholesome even while she angles her top down to the third button.

First photo: angled overhead. Cheekbones and cleavage. Glowing skin under a filter named after a Parisian street she'll never visit.

Second: her and a dog that's clearly not hers. No fur in her apartment pics, no bowls, no leash.

Third: mirror selfie at the gym. Tight leggings, sports bra, fake humility in the caption: "Not bad for a Monday, right?"

Fourth: wine glass in hand, staring out a window, pretending to be deep.

Fifth: her in bed, "just woke up" hair that took 30 minutes to style.

Bio: Lover of crime podcasts & red wine Gym rat Social media strategist (freelance) Not here for hookups lol In the city but missing the country

I feel the sneer creep into my jaw. Every word, every emoji—scripted. Practiced.

I stare at her message a little longer than necessary. Not because I need time to think—because I want the tone to be **perfect**.

Charming. Familiar. Non-threatening. The kind of guy she thinks she wants.

I type:

> ***Me:*** *"Haha, maybe—unless I've just been admiring you from afar Either way, not a bad way to meet again."*

Send.

Casual. Warm. Harmless. On the surface.

What she doesn't realize is that I've already adjusted my location radius to match her exact block. Already scanned her photos for EXIF data. Already scraped metadata off her profile link.

She thinks this is a flirt. But I'm inside her digital walls now. I'll be inside her pink wet walls later.

She's typing again. Three dots. Pause. Typing. Delete. Typing again. She's already curating her next response.

Good.

If she's editing herself for me, that means she wants to be seen. She wants to be touched, owned by me.

And I'm going to see **everything**.

She's the same girl who laughed when I spilled my tray freshman year, but now she's edited herself into something marketable. Digestible.

She thinks she's in control here. She has no idea the moment she matched me... the moment she sent that message...**her life stopped belonging to her.**

I let my finger hover over the reply button. Be careful what you ask for, Lily. You're about to get very familiar.

Lily Grant. Unaware. Untouched. Alive. The ribbon for her is still unwritten.

I smile. Not the kind you share. The kind that bares teeth in the dark.

CHAPTER TWO

Fist Contact

Her second message lands with a little notification chime—so innocuous it could almost be funny.

> ***Lily:*** *"Haha, well, if you've been admiring me, I'm flattered. You look like trouble in a good way. "*

I stare at the words. The emoji. The practiced warmth.

Trouble in a good way. That's how she sees me already—a curated fantasy. She has no idea how accurate she is.

I roll my shoulders back and type, letting the persona slide on like an old suit.

> ***Me:*** *"Trouble might be my specialty. Though you don't seem like the type to scare easily."*

Send.

It's strange how easily I slip into this role. Charming. Teasing. Safe. The perfect man behind the glass. Every reply is a probe. Every little laugh emoji, every ellipsis before she hits send, is another data point for her file.

She's typing again. She stops. Deletes. Starts over. Hesitation. Insecurity.

I smile.

Good.

While I wait for her next message, I open her Instagram. Her feed is a graveyard of carefully staged snapshots—her in yoga poses, her in tight dresses, her with that same wine glass like it's some talisman of authenticity.

A persona made of filters and desperation.

She's posted six stories in the last twelve hours. Half selfies. Half a dozen little videos with captions like *"Self-care Sunday"* and *"Strong women lift each other."*

I almost laugh.

You've been lifting yourself up for years, haven't you, Lily? But here you are, aching for someone to take the weight off your shoulders.

I can do that.

Her next message pops up:

> ***Lily:*** *"Definitely not scared. So … what's your story? You seem interesting."*

A question. She's inviting me in. She doesn't realize she's holding the door wide open.

I lean back in my chair, savoring the moment. This is how it always starts: curiosity. Curiosity becomes interest. Interest becomes trust. Trust becomes ownership.

She has no idea she's already mine.

I type, measured, and warm:

> ***Me:*** *"I work in security consulting—corporate risk, boring stuff mostly. Moved here a couple of years ago. I'm probably a little*

too into late-night gym sessions and crime documentaries. You?"

The irony isn't lost on me. Risk management. Security.

She types back fast:

Lily: *"Oh my God, I'm a true crime junkie too. If you're not careful, I'll talk your ear off about unsolved cases. "*

I close my eyes, let her voice fill the space behind my forehead. She's already opening up and already imagining the version of me she wants to see.

I can be that. I can be anything Lilly needs—until she needs nothing at all.

I open the folder on my desktop titled **Target-32-LG**. I drag her photos into it, one by one. I label each: *Day One Contact.*

Then I pull up her address. The GPS ping I lifted from her phone is precise to within 3 meters. Her building. Her floor. Her door.

I click the screen off and smile in the dark. First contact is the easiest part. The part all women think they control.

They never do.

CHAPTER THREE

Stalking in Plain Sight

The first date is set for Friday night. A wine bar she picked—some place with exposed brick and Edison bulbs, the kind of atmosphere that feels curated for Instagram stories.

Me: *"It looks cozy,"*

It will be. I'll make sure of it.

Before Friday, there were things I needed to know—routines, patterns, vulnerabilities. Every detail she thought no one noticed.

The first night, I followed her home. She parked in the south corner of the garage, the darkest spot—lazy or confident, I wasn't sure. The elevator was always empty by the time she got there. She unlocked her door with one hand, phone in the other, keys dangling between her fingers like some halfhearted weapon.

I watched her from the shadows, noting every habit. She double-checked the deadbolt but never the sliding window by the fire escape. She left the kitchen light on. She kicked off her shoes at the threshold, like she was shedding her day.

I cataloged it all. She didn't know I was there. That I was closer than any stranger had a right to be. Closer than the people she thought she trusted.

The second night, I waited until she was asleep before I moved. Her car was the easiest target—clean, new, predictable. I slipped the tracker behind the rear fender, my gloved hands steady as my heartbeat.

I ran my fingertips along the polished paint—an intimate touch she would never feel. But I would.

I circled the car once before leaving, just to admire it—her space, her scent lingering in the upholstery, the receipts tucked in the door pocket. She had gone to a juice bar that morning— twelve dollars on something green and self-righteous. And now she's in bed, dreaming of Friday and dreaming of me.

I wonder what version of me she imagines. What tidy narrative she's building to explain the way she feels when I text her, when I tease her just enough to keep her wanting more.

She wants to believe she's safe. That the man she matched with is exactly who he says he is. She has no idea she's already under glass. Already pinned in place.

Back in my apartment, I bring up the tracker's dashboard. A little red dot glows on the map. Her. Always her. I close my eyes and picture her sleeping. Picture the way she'll look on Friday when I hold her hand across the table, when she thanks me for being such a gentleman.

And I smile.

Because while she's dreaming of connection, of possibility, I'm dreaming of the moment her last illusion dies.

Soon.

CHAPTER FOUR

The First Date

She's already seated when I arrive—table by the window, candlelight low and deliberate, making her skin glow until it looks almost edible. Her phone lies face down, forgotten. Chosen. Her hair is tucked behind one ear like she expects to be watched.

The dress clings to her in all the right places. Thin spaghetti straps barely committed to their duty, resting on the curve of her shoulders like an invitation waiting for the right hands. Her neckline dips just enough to distract—soft flesh, shadowed heat, the promise of what she thinks she's controlling.

My eyes linger longer than they should on her perfectly plump breasts. Long enough to picture those straps slipping and my tongue sliding down her neck and onto her chest, flicking her nipples. Long enough to imagine how easily she'd let them fall if I asked the right way.

She shifts in her seat, crosses her legs, oblivious—or pretending to be. The movement makes my jaw tighten. Makes restraint feel like a choice instead of an instinct. Not yet, I remind myself. This part is about anticipation. About letting her believe she's the one deciding how far this goes.

I take my seat across from her, meet her smile, and lock everything else away. For now.

Her smile when she spots me is almost shy. I wonder if she practiced it in the mirror. "Hi." Her voice is lighter in person, almost girlish. Like she's trying to pretend this is nothing. Just a date. Just a possibility.

I step closer, lean in as if the noise requires it, and press a hand lightly to her shoulder. "Hi," I echo. "You look...incredible."

She blushes. Just the way I thought she would. A flush of pink crept up her neck. I sit across from her, one hand folded on the table. Open. Relaxed. Exactly the posture I know makes women feel safe. She doesn't realize I've already memorized her. Doesn't know that before I even walked in, I sat in my car and watched her through the window, observing the way she stirred her wine, the way she kept glancing at the door. Practiced nervousness. The performance of vulnerability.

"Traffic was a nightmare," I say. She laughs softly, brushing her thumb across the rim of her glass.

"You made it. That's what matters."

I tilt my head, studying the slope of her throat. It's not the wine she's tasting when she looks at me. It's the story she's telling herself: that this is fate, or chemistry, or some other lie she's addicted to.

We order. Small plates she can pretend to pick at while she talks. She asks questions—about my work, my family, what brought me here. I give her just enough truth to be credible.

"My mom used to say I was too serious," I say, smiling. "I guess I haven't grown out of that."

She reaches across the table and lets her fingers rest on the back of my hand. A delicate touch that makes her feel brave. She has no idea I can feel her pulse just beneath her skin. Her phone buzzes once. She ignores it.

"You're not what I expected," she murmurs.

I arch a brow. "What did you expect?"

She shakes her head, looking away like she's embarrassed. "I don't know. Someone more ... self-absorbed? You're very ... present."

If she only knew how true that was. "You make it easy," I say.

She smiles again, and it's softer this time. Real. Or as real as anything she offers.

She doesn't notice how carefully I watch her. How I track every twitch of her mouth when she lies—like when she says she's single because she's too focused on work, when it's really because she's terrified no one will stay. How she lifts her glass to her lips to buy time when a question lands too close to something she's hiding.

The check comes. I insist. Another performance. Another way to smooth her defenses.

Outside, she hugs me—tight, warm, lingering.

"Text me when you get home?" she says.

I nod, brushing my lips against her hair. "I will."

She walks to her car, heels clicking on the pavement. I stand and watch until she unlocks the door, until she's inside and the engine turns over.

I don't text her when I get home. I don't have to.

I already know exactly where she's going. Exactly what time she'll slip out of that dress. Exactly how she'll look in the dark.

I turn away and smile. She has no idea this was never a first date.

It was an introduction to the end.

CHAPTER FIVE

The Listening Room

I call it the Listening Room. It isn't a room, exactly—just a part of my apartment where I've arranged the monitors, the drives, the files—a shrine made of glass and data.

Tonight, her living room glows across four screens. One angle from the hallway camera, I piggybacked on the building's security feed. One from the webcam she never bothered to cover.Two from the tiny devices I tucked into the corners of her bedroom when she left the window cracked for fresh air. The bedroom ones are my favorite. I get to watch her undress, pleasure herself, and imagine what it will be like when I run my hands along every inch of her body.

People are always so careless when they think no one is watching.

She doesn't know she's performing for me right now. Every flick of her hair. Every stretch of her legs across the couch. Every sigh when she scrolls through her phone and finds nothing satisfying enough to hold her attention. I'll satisfy her soon enough. Soon enough, she will be sighing from pleasure as I run my tongue along the inner parts of her thighs, up into the folds of her labia, and when I find her pleasure center, I'll make sure she is held in place long enough to make her remember who she belongs to.

I can hear her breathing. Hear the glass when she sets it on the table. Hear her voice when she makes the call she'll regret later.

Her friend's voice comes on the speaker. **"So? How was it?"**

Lily laughs, low and self-conscious. "Better than I expected."

"Tell me everything."

She does.

Her friend laughs softly on speaker—warm, tired, wine-loose. "Safe? Girl, that alone puts him above ninety percent of the men in this city."

Lily sinks deeper into her couch, curling her legs under herself. She looks small like that—almost girlish. "I know. It's stupid. But the way he listens? I don't feel like I'm performing with him."

Performing. She has no idea that's all she is doing.

Her friend exhales, glass clinking. "You deserve that, girl. You deserve someone who sees you."

Lily's voice cracks so quietly I almost miss it. "I'm scared to trust it. I don't want to screw it up."

My pulse kicks. Screw it up? Sweetheart, the screw already happened. You just haven't noticed where the threads lead.

Her friend asks, "Do you like him? Actually like him?"

Lily hesitates—and I lean forward instinctively, waiting.

"...Yeah," she whispers. "I really do. When I was with him, it felt like my brain finally shut up. Like I could breathe."

Her friend makes a soft noise of approval. "That's rare."

Lily laughs under her breath. Nervous. "Or delusional."

"You're allowed to want good things."

Lily rubs her forehead. She looks exhausted—emotionally hungover by hope. "I just ... I don't know. There's something about him. Something that feels familiar."

My eyes close. There it is.

Her friend perks up. "Familiar how?"

Lily shakes her head, staring at the darkness of her living room like it might give her answers. "Like I've met him before. Or dreamed him. I can't explain it."

My breath drags low in my throat. She remembers the echo— not the source.

Her friend teases lightly, "A past-life soulmate?"

Lily smiles, whisper-soft. "Maybe. All I know is ... I want to see him again."

My hand curls into a fist—not in anger, but in victory.

Her friend yawns. "Then stop overthinking. Just enjoy it. You deserve a man who makes you feel safe."

Safe. God, if she only knew.

When Lily hangs up, she stands in front of the window and looks out across the city lights like she's searching for a sign. She doesn't know that I'm staring back. That she is already surrounded. Already drowning in me.

And she whispers to the empty room— voice trembling with desire, she doesn't understand: "I hope he texts."

I smile at the monitor. Oh, Lily. I won't text. I'll be at your door.

I smile at the screen. It's not amusement. It's possession. I switch to the bedroom feed as she changes. Her dress pools around her ankles, and the camera captures every angle. She stretches, unselfconscious, unguarded. The sight of her like this—oblivious, vulnerable—sinks into me like a blade sliding home, the same way I'll slide into her very soon..

I open the folder I started after our first date.

Target-32-LG.

Inside:

- The photo I took of her walking to her car.
- Screenshots of every message she's sent me.

- Audio clips of her voice when she thinks she's alone.

I add another piece to the file. Tonight's footage. And the earring.

It sits on the desk in front of me—gold, delicate, warm from her skin when I took it. She'll think she lost it somewhere between the restaurant and her apartment. She'll search her purse. Check the car. But she won't find it.

It's mine now.

Just like she is.

CHAPTER SIX

The Second Date

The second date is easier. It always is. Once they decide you're safe, you don't have to work as hard to pretend. They fill in the gaps for themselves—make excuses for what you don't say, turn your silences into something romantic instead of calculated manipulation.

Lily arrives five minutes early. Her hair is pulled back, and she's dressed casual but chosen carefully enough to look effortless. She lights up when she sees me. Her smile is bright, open. So trusting it makes my pulse slow with satisfaction.

"Hi." She steps close, hugging me like we've known each other longer than a week. "I hope I didn't keep you waiting," she says against my shoulder.

"You're right on time," I reply.

She pulls back, smiling as if she believes me. We sit. Menus between us. Candlelight. The illusion of romance was so thick I could bottle it. She tucks a curl behind her ear. "Today was insane. One of my clients sent edits at three a.m. and expected them back by sunrise."

I hum, letting the sound encourage her.

"I swear, people think working from home means I'm just ... available constantly."

"That sounds exhausting," I say. It doesn't matter what I say—she just needs somewhere to put her words.

She laughs—small, apologetic. "Sorry. I don't mean to unload. I just—"

"You can talk to me." And she does.

"My best friend hasn't replied to a single message all week," she continues, stabbing at the ice in her water glass. "And my mom left me on read. I feel like I'm just ... yelling into a void sometimes." She forces a smile. "God, listen to me. Second date and I'm already an emotional disaster."

I shake my head. "No. You're being honest."

Her shoulders loosen. She looks down, voice dropping to something close to the truth. "I think people forget I'm human, you know? Like I'm only useful if I'm working or helping somebody else." She glances up at me carefully. "Have you ever felt that way?"

"More times than you'd believe." The answer satisfies her.

She exhales, fingers playing with the edge of her napkin. "I don't usually open up like this. I don't know why I am now."

I lean in just enough. "Maybe because you want to be seen."

Her breath catches. "Yeah," she whispers. "Yeah, maybe."

She looks away quickly, cheeks pink. "Sorry, I'm talking too much."

"You're not."

She smiles again, and this time it reaches her eyes.

Then, softer—almost shy: "You make it easy. Being around you."

I give a slow nod, and even I can hear how gentle my reply sounds: "I like hearing you."

And it's true— not the words. The cracks between them. The loneliness she mistakes for depth. The hunger she mistakes for connection.

Her voice smooths out, warmer now: "It just feels good to talk to someone who listens."

If she only knew. I'm not listening to what she says. I'm memorizing the map beneath it.

I reach across the table, brushing her wrist with my fingers. Her pulse flutters. She doesn't pull away. She leans into it. Her lips part as if she's about to say something vulnerable, but she swallows it back. Instead, she gives me a shy, conspiratorial smile. Like we share some secret no one else could understand.

She has no idea how right she is.

When the food comes, I watch her carefully. How she picks at her plate, how she glances up through her lashes when she laughs. Every reaction cataloged. Every movement added to the profile I'm building in my mind. This is the moment most men ruin it—by pushing too hard, showing too much hunger too soon. I let the hunger stay just behind my eyes, softened by a smile. It's more effective that way.

Halfway through the meal, I let my knee brush hers under the table. The contact makes her breath hitch, and I can't help but watch her breasts rise and fall. She doesn't move away." Sorry," I murmur.

She shakes her head, her cheeks flushed. "Don't be."

I keep my leg there. I let the pressure build in the silence, the way I imagine the soft folds between her legs is becoming wet.

When the check comes, she insists on splitting it. A little show of independence, she thinks, makes her less predictable.

It doesn't.

Outside, I walk her to her car. The night is cold, the air sharp with the promise of rain. She looks up at me, her eyes bright in the glow of the parking lot lights. "This was ... really nice," she says softly.

I step closer, close enough to see the way her pulse flutters in her throat. I don't kiss her. Not yet. Instead, I lift my hand and tuck a strand of hair behind her ear. Let my thumb brush the edge of her jaw and hold myself back from ripping her clothes off right there and taking her across the car, thrashing her as hard as I can.

She sways closer, her breath catching.

"Text me when you get home," I say.

She nods, like she can't quite find her voice. *Not yet lily, I'll make you speechless soon enough.* She doesn't know that before she even pulls out of the lot, I'll be behind her. Doesn't know I'll watch her unlock her door, watch her lights come on, watch her move through her apartment with the same trust she's giving me now.

Doesn't know she's already mine.

CHAPTER SEVEN

Isolation Games

It starts with small things.

A message that never delivers. A call that drops before it connects. A calendar invite that quietly disappears.

Lily thinks it's her phone. Or the apps. Perhaps bad luck.

It's none of those. I learned early that the easiest way to isolate someone isn't to frighten them—it's to inconvenience them. To erode their connections grain by grain until they don't notice they're standing alone. By the time they realize, it feels inevitable. Natural.

I watch her through the monitors. She sits on the couch, phone in hand, thumb scrolling old texts she swears she replied to. Her mouth moves as she mutters to herself, confusion creasing her brow. There's a little frown when her best friend doesn't answer her calls. The way she checks her email again and again, hoping to see something she never will, sends a tickle up my spine.

I deleted it. I deleted all of it. The apologies she'll never read. The invitations she'll never see. The small reassurances that might have reminded her she's not alone.

I lean back in my chair and close my eyes, listening to her voice on the speakers.

> **Lily:** "Hey, it's me again. Just wondering if you got my text…I guess you're busy. Call me?"

She sounds tired. A little frayed at the edges. Perfect.

When she finally sets her phone aside, she picks up the glass of wine she's been nursing all night and stares into it like she expects to find answers there. It's almost tender, watching her start to come undone. Not in a sudden, violent way. But slowly—like a fabric unraveling under a patient hand. When she finally reaches for her laptop, I already know what she's about to do. She opens our messages.

Me. The only thread she can still hold onto. Her fingers hover over the keys before she types.

Lily: *Hey.*

A pause. Then:

Lily: *Can we talk?*

I don't answer right away. I let the typing indicator appear—then disappear. I let her check the clock. I let her sip her wine too fast. I want her to feel the space where everyone else used to be.

When I finally reply, it's simple.

Me: *Of course. I'm here.*

The relief hits her instantly. I see it in the way her shoulders drop, in the way she exhales like she's been holding her breath for hours. I can't ignore that she has picked her silky pajama bottoms for tonight's wine session. They always ride up and show most of her ass. When she bends over, I get a glance of what I will be slipping into soon enough.

Lily: *Thank you.*

Lily: *I don't know what's wrong with everything lately.*

I wait. Let her fill the silence.

Lily: *It feels like people just keep… slipping away.*

Lily: *Like I'm doing something wrong.*

I tilt my head, watching her through the monitor. Watching as she leans forward, positions the computer so she's lying on her stomach now. I switch the camera so I can see down her tank top, and her breasts are fully exposed. The round nipples pressing against the couch and her shorts ride up, exposing the bottom of her cheeks where I'll be running my tongue along sooner than she realizes.

Me: *You're not doing anything wrong.*

Me: *Sometimes people just don't show up the way they should.*

Her reply comes faster now.

Lily: *That's what I keep telling myself.*

Lily: *But it's hard not to feel stupid for caring.*

I lean forward, resting my elbows on the desk, and I rub the growing bulge in my pants. Lily has no idea what she does to me.

Me: *Caring isn't stupid.*

Me: *It's rare.*

She bites her lip. I know she does—I've memorized the habit. I've memorized most of her habits now. I can't wait to find out which ones she has when I'm pounding into her and making her scream my name.

Lily: *You always know what to say.*

Lily: *I feel calmer when I talk to you.*

There it is. I type slowly, deliberately.

Me: *That's because I'm listening.*

Me: *You don't have to pretend with me.*

Another pause. Longer this time.

Lily: *Can I ask you something?*

I smile. Hoping this is when she asks me to join her on that couch, and the wait is over. I no longer have to handle myself; I want her mouth to take over.

Me: *Anything.*

Lily: *Do you think people leave because they see the real you?*

Lily: *Or because they never really wanted to stay?*

I don't hesitate.

Me: *They leave because they don't deserve access to you.*

Her eyes shine at the screen.

Lily: *I'm really glad I met you.*

My fingers hover over the keys with my left hand, and my right hand is wrapped around my cock, stroking up and down with a fever I can barely control.

Me: *So am I.*

And she believes it— that this connection is organic. That this comfort is mutual. She doesn't know that the man she's clinging to is the one who made the world feel so thin in the first place.

She doesn't know how easy it was to become her only constant.

And she never will.

CHAPTER EIGHT

THE BREACH

THE LOCK YIELDS WITH almost no resistance. A slight turn of the pick, a soft click. It's obscene how easy it is to slip into her life. I know it will be easier to slip inside of her when the time comes. I'll slip inside every hole she has soon enough.

I step inside and close the door behind me, breathing in the stale warmth of her apartment. Even here, she performs—candles arranged in curated clusters. Throw blankets folded just so. A life manicured into something she hopes will look enviable if anyone ever looks too close.

She has no idea I'm already the closest anyone has ever been.

The monitors back in my apartment show her bedroom, but they don't capture this—the weight of the air, the sound of her breathing, the truth of how close I am. Watching her in person is better.

She's asleep, tangled in a thin sheet, one arm flung over her head. Her mouth slightly opens in a soft exhale, and it's all I can do not to unzip my pants and jerk off right in front of her. I walk past the couch, trailing gloved fingers along the back of it, then into the kitchen. I open a cabinet, scan the neat rows of glasses and mugs. I pick one up and hold it for a moment before setting it back in the same spot.

A ritual. A claiming.

I pause in her doorway, watching the quiet rise and fall of her chest. The sound of her breathing steadies me—not with peace, but with certainty. She belongs to me in this moment. She just hasn't agreed to it yet. I could take her now, but I won't. I want her to invite me in, to choose me the first time. Because once she does—once she chooses me—there's no closing that door again. Like a vampire, I only need permission once.

She shifts in her sleep, her brow knitting. A flicker of discomfort crosses her face, like some part of her can feel me in the room. She won't remember it in the morning. She'll dismiss it as a dream.

I cross the floor, slow and deliberate. At the foot of the bed, her jewelry lies in a small ceramic dish. I chose a bracelet. Gold, delicate, studded with tiny green stones, she wears on days she wants to feel pretty. She wore it the first night we met in person. I slip it into my pocket. Something hers. Something she'll look for later without knowing exactly when she lost it.

She stirs again, murmuring something unintelligible. I leave the bedroom as silently as I entered. I retrace my steps, lock the door behind me, and stand in the hallway for a moment, feeling the echo of her presence cling to me.

This is the point of no return. The moment the story becomes real. The threshold crossed—hers and mine.

Back in my apartment, I set the bracelet on the highest shelf of my shrine. Next to the earring. Next to the photos. I stare at it, breathing evenly, until the adrenaline stops pulsing through my veins.

She doesn't yet know she belongs to me.

But she will.

CHAPTER NINE

The Confession Mirror

It starts with a text.

> **ME:** *Rough day? You were quiet earlier.*

Simple. Concern disguised as curiosity. She doesn't realize it's the first tug on a string I tightened weeks ago.

Three dots appear. Disappear. Reappear.

I wait. Patience is something she's taught me without meaning to. Her hesitation has become familiar.

> **Lily:** *Yeah. Just ... stuff. I don't really want to talk about it.*

Perfect. I call before she can retreat. The line rings once, twice—then she answers.

Lily: "Hey,"

Lily: "Sorry. I'm just … tired."

I soften my voice, shape it into the man she believes she chose.

Me: "You don't have to apologize. You can talk to me. You know that."

A pause. Then a breath that isn't steady.

Lily: "I don't know why I'm like this,"

Me: "Like what?"

Lily: "Always waiting for it to fall apart. Like if I let myself be happy, it'll just get taken away."

I tap the recorder and watch the red dot appear. Her voice feeds into my headphones while her image fills the monitor in front of me—real, immediate. She's curled on her bed just like I knew she would be, phone pressed to her cheek, one knee drawn in. The lamp is on. It always is when she's unsettled. I see the tension in her mouth, the way her fingers worry at the edge of the blanket. She has no idea how visible she is.

Lily: "I've never told anyone that,"

I don't respond right away. I watch her swallow. Watch her blink too fast. Sometimes silence pulls harder than words.

Lily: "Sometimes I think I'm broken," Like there's something wrong with me that can't be fixed."

There's a tightness in my chest—not empathy. Recognition. The satisfaction of seeing her reflected exactly where I want her.

Me: "You're not broken,"

She gives a small, shaky laugh. "

Lily: You don't even know me."

My eyes don't leave the screen.

Me: "I know enough."

Silence again. She shifts on the bed, curling tighter, like she's bracing for something she doesn't know is already decided.

Then—

Lily: "Do you want to come over?"

Lily: "I don't want to be alone tonight."

There it is. The invitation. I don't smile. I don't rush. I let the moment settle into place. This isn't impulse—it's confirmation. She opened the door herself.

Me: "I can be there,"

Me: "If that's what you want."

She nods before she realizes I can't see her, at least that's what she thinks. Then she says,

Lily: "Yes. I want that."

I end the call and stand, already reaching for my jacket, my eyes still on the monitor and my hand adjusting myself, trying to keep calm.

She thinks she asked for comfort. She thinks she made the choice. But mirrors don't lie. And tonight, she invited me in.

She answers the door after a single knock, like she was waiting for me. Her eyes are red, glassy—the aftermath of tears she didn't bother hiding. Good. I need her soft tonight, not uncertain.

I take her hand gently, enough to steady her, and draw her into me. My arm folds around her shoulders, my fingers brushing through her hair as if I'm soothing something fragile. I tell her she isn't alone, that I'm here, and guide us backward while my foot nudges the door closed.

She trembles against me, breath hitching as fresh tears soak into my shoulder. I've got her.

We sit on the couch. She pulls away just enough to swipe at her face, embarrassed by the evidence she left on my jacket. I tilt my head, keep my voice low. "You don't have to perform for me," I say. "Let it go. Tell me everything."

Her hands twist together.

Lily: "I don't understand why everyone leaves,

Lily: "I feel so alone. Thank you for coming tonight. It means everything to me."

She has no idea what those words cost her. How it means more to me than she could ever imagine. Tonight, she gives herself to me piece by piece, believing she's choosing comfort. Believing she's safe.

I lean forward and press a kiss to her forehead, slow and deliberate. "There's nowhere else I'd rather be."

She looks at me then—really looks at me—and something inside her settles. Lily lifts her hands to my face, her fingers warm and trusting, and kisses me.

I pull back just enough to meet her eyes. "Are you sure?"

Her nod is small but certain. Those wide eyes never leave mine. That's all I need. I close the distance, slide my arms around her waist, and draw her in completely—no space, no doubt, no turning back.

I let her think she closed the distance. Her kiss deepens, turns hungry, and for a moment she moves first—hands sliding, mouth demanding, confidence blooming now that I've stopped pretending to lead. I allow it. Control doesn't require urgency. Control requires certainty.

Her fingers fist in my jacket like she's anchoring herself. Like if she lets go, she'll drift away.

I don't touch her right away. That's when she notices. She pulls back just enough to look at me, breath quick, pupils blown wide. "You're thinking," she says, not accusing—curious. Challenging.

"I'm listening," I reply.

That's a lie. I'm watching the way she squares her shoulders, the way something darker stirs beneath the vulnerability she showed me earlier. Grief didn't hollow her out—it sharpened her. She wants to be taken, yes. But she also wants to take.

Good.

She presses me back against the couch, deliberate now, fingers tracing slow lines over my chest like she's learning the shape of power. I stay still. Let her have the illusion. Let her feel bold. She starts to dig her fingernails into me, and my back arches in pleasure.

Her mouth finds my ear. "I don't want you to be gentle," she whispers.

The words land exactly where I expected them to. Right at the center of my core.

My hands slide to her hips—not to pull her closer, but to hold her there. Stop her. Remind her I'm still here. Still watching. Still deciding.

"Then tell me what you want," I say quietly.

She doesn't hesitate. She tells me.

"I want you to take me—take me as you've never taken anyone before. I want you to slide your cock inside my pussy slowly, then start pounding me until I feel every single inch of you inside me. I want you to spank me, slap me, slam me up against a wall, and then slam me back down onto the bed. I want you to tie me up and have your way with me until I scream your name. I want you to completely dominate me, and when you break me, I want you to let me break you."

And I realize, with distant fascination, that the girl on my monitor—the one who cried and curled inward—is gone. In her place is something reckless. Hungry. Willing to burn if it means not feeling empty.

She straddles the space between us like she's claiming ground, her mouth finding mine again, this time with intent. Teeth. Heat. Demand. I let my hands finally move. Inside, I feel nothing rise but satisfaction.

This isn't connection. This isn't passion. This is consent wrapping itself around inevitability. She thinks she's leading now. Thinks she's choosing darkness because it feels better than fear. I let her believe it. Because victory doesn't always look like force. Sometimes it looks like letting her climb straight into the fire—and calling it hers.

She wraps her small, manicured fingers around my bulging erection and guides me inside her folds. She's so wet I can feel her juices drip onto my groin. She's warm—almost hot. She rocks her hips back and forth, but I stop her, throw her down onto the bed, and her eyes go wide.

"Not yet," I say. "I need to feed first."

She smiles wickedly, knowing I'll be burying my face in her pussy and ass now, but she has no idea that when she climaxes, I won't stop there. I open her pussy lips and flick her clit with my tongue. Her back arches like a gymnast attempting a gold-medal backbend. I fill my mouth with her, my tongue licking her up and down, my lips moving from top to bottom, right under her vaginal opening.

Her eyes go wide, like she can't believe I'm eating her this way. She's never had someone like me—they never do.

"Oh my God, please don't stop. Please."

Oh, Lily. I won't. I'm going to make sure you tremble beneath my touch in more ways than you could ever imagine.

I feel her climax in my mouth. Her legs clamp around my ears. She tries to push my head away, but I don't stop. She starts to crawl up the bed, trying to escape, but I grab her hips and continue burying my face deep into her folds, pushing my index finger into her asshole. She jumps and screams in ecstasy, clamping a hand over her mouth.

There it is—the moment I know I broke her. And now it's my turn.

I release my grip, pull my finger from her ass, and wipe it on her blanket. Then I thrust my cock into her, grabbing her shoulders. I make sure I can feel the bottom of her vaginal walls as I pound her until she can barely breathe. She's wincing now—afraid of the pain even as she enjoys it.

I slow down for a moment and let her catch her breath.

"You are amazing," she says. "I can't believe how good this feels."

I slam into her harder and make her scream—a scream she didn't realize she'd enjoy. She grabs my nipples and pushes me back.

"My turn."

I lie down and let her mount me.

"Turn around," I tell her. "I want to watch your ass bounce on me."

She smiles like a Cheshire cat and obliges. Her ass is perfectly heart-shaped, and I watch my dick slide in and out of her tight pussy. She's good at what she does—but I'm better. I'll let her finish me this time. Next time, I'll fuck her mouth just as hard as I fucked her pussy.

It doesn't take long. Watching her ass bounce does the trick. I release my load inside her, and she stays there, catching her breath while my body gives its small, involuntary jerks.

"I can't believe I forgot to make you wear a condom."

"It's okay," I say. "I've been tested regularly since I became sexually active. I'm also sterile—from a childhood accident—so there's no risk of pregnancy."

I lie, making her comfortable. None of it matters.

I know she'll want to cuddle now. I'll let her. She needs to feel safe. Her dark side needs to be balanced with her soft one—or she won't let it surface again.

CHAPTER TEN

THE ABDUCTION

SHE DOESN'T STRUGGLE AT first. That's the thing no one tells you— In the beginning, there's only confusion. A split-second when their brain tries to slot the moment into something familiar, something survivable.

The soft voice—mine—calling her name. The way I step inside like I've always belonged there.

She blinks up at me from the couch, her face flushed from the glass of wine she poured to help her sleep. Her mouth opens in a question she never gets to finish.

I cross the room and press my palm to her cheek. Gentle. Reassuring. Like a lover's caress.

"Shh," I whisper.

And then the cloth is over her mouth. The scent—chemical, heavy—fills the space between us.

Her eyes go wide. She tries to pull back, but my arm is already around her shoulders, holding her against my chest. For a heartbeat, she looks at me like she knows me. Really knows me. Not the man I pretended to be. The man I am. Like she always suspected, there was something about me she should be careful about, but her HOPE kept moving forward.

Her pupils dilate. Her body shudders.

It's not rage that drives me in that moment. Not vengeance. Its purpose. The same calm that settles over me when I set a blade against skin. The same certainty that comes when I collect the final piece of the game.

Her limbs grow heavy. Her breath slows. I ease her down onto the floor, cradling her head so she doesn't bruise. Her eyelids flutter, then still. I brush the hair back from her forehead. Trace the curve of her cheek with my thumb. I stop there, I have no desire to touch her intimate parts without her looking at me, knowing who's doing it.

"You did so well," I murmur.

She doesn't hear me. But that's all right. This was always how it was meant to be.

I lift her carefully, feeling the weight of her body settle against mine. Her head rests against my shoulder, her hair soft against my throat. Intimate. Like a dance. Like a promise kept.

I carry her through the doorway, past the life she built for strangers to admire, into the dark.

This is a ritual—a velvet snare closing around the last of her freedom.

And I have never felt more alive.

CHAPTER ELEVEN

THE LAIR

LILY WAKES IN PIECES. Confused about her whereabouts, lost on what happened.

First, the sound—low and resonant, like a heartbeat pulsing through hidden speakers. Then the smell—warm leather, clean linen, something darker beneath it. Finally, the light—soft and golden, spilling across her face in a way that almost feels gentle.

She blinks, lashes clumping with tears she doesn't remember shedding. Her mouth is dry, wrists bound, velvet straps pressing into her skin—firm, intentional. For a moment, she thinks it's a dream. Some twisted nightmare that will dissolve if she closes her eyes again.

But when she shifts, she feels it—the meticulous restraints, the cool air licking across exposed skin. She's wearing nothing but underwear. Someone undressed her. He undressed her.

A soft click breaks the hush. Footsteps. Measured. Unhurried.

When she looks up, he's standing in the doorway.

Ethan.

He looks the same—jeans, black shirt, calm expression as if he's walked in to share coffee instead of … this.

"Good morning," he says, voice warm and conversational.

Lily tries to swallow. Her throat burns. He tilts his head, studying her like a fascinating specimen under glass.

"You don't have to speak yet," he continues. "Just listen." He steps closer. The shadows seem to shift around him, like they belong to him. "You're safe," he says softly. "Safe here with me."

Her heart stutters in her chest, frantic and useless.

His gaze slides over her—slow, proprietary. "I know you're scared." He kneels beside the bed, resting his forearms against the mattress. "But I promise you, Lily ... you've never been safer. Because now you don't have to pretend anymore."

She wants to scream, but the sound dies in her throat.

"Do you remember," he murmurs, "the night you told me you felt broken inside?"

Her breath shudders.

"I remember," he whispers. "I remember everything you've ever said to me."

She shakes her head, tears slipping down her temples. "This is insane," she manages. Her voice is hoarse. "You're insane."

His lips curve into something that isn't quite a smile. "Maybe," he says. "Or maybe this is the most honest thing either of us has ever done." He reaches out, brushing her cheek with his knuckles. The touch is so tender that it twists her stomach.

"You told me you liked feeling helpless," he says softly. "You liked it when someone else was in control."

She squeezes her eyes shut. "That's not—" The word collapses under the weight of her confusion, because part of her remembers saying it. Remembers meaning it. Remembers wanting the dark edges of surrender. She hates herself for the way her skin prickles under his touch. For the way her pulse stutters when he leans in, his breath warm against her ear.

“You’re home now,” he murmurs. “Where you belong.”

Lily doesn’t know if she’s crying hard from terror—or from the awful, undeniable truth that part of her doesn’t want to look away.

CHAPTER TWELVE

THE UNVEILING

LILY HAS ALMOST STOPPED crying by the time he comes back.

Almost.

The door opens without a sound, and for a moment she thinks it's a hallucination—a trick of her exhausted mind. But then he steps into the light. The mask covers the lower half of his face. Matte black. Seamless. Intimate in a way that makes her skin crawl. She doesn't recognize it, and somehow that's worse than seeing him bare-faced. It erases whatever small familiarity she clung to.

"Good," he says quietly. "You're awake, we can finally have some fun."

She doesn't respond. She doesn't trust her voice not to break. She doesn't want to give him that. He carries a small wooden box, polished to a dull sheen. He sets it on the table beside the bed, then pulls up a chair and turns it so he can watch her fully. Not like a man sitting—but like someone settling in.

"I want to show you something," he murmurs. He lifts the lid. Her stomach rolls. Inside is her earring. The gold bracelet she thought she'd lost. A folded napkin with the name of the wine bar from their first date. A lock of hair, bound with a thin red thread.

Her vision blurs. "No," she whispers, before her voice gives out. "No—"

"Yes." His voice is soft. Almost kind. "I've been keeping pieces of you for a long time." He lifts the earring, rolling it between his gloved fingers. "You wore this the first night you let me touch you," he says. "Do you remember? You smiled when I brushed your wrist."

Her head shakes against the pillow as tears slide down her temples. She can't stop them. She doesn't try.

"You think you didn't choose this," he continues, his voice low and hypnotic. "But you did."

"You're sick," she manages to choke out.

"Maybe," he agrees easily. "But so are you."

He sets the earring back inside the box and reaches for a small recorder. Clicks it on. Her own voice fills the room—cracked, tired, heartbreakingly familiar.

I don't know why I'm like this. Sometimes I think I'm broken. Will you stay on the phone? Just for a little while...

She turns her face away, shame and horror knotting inside her like a living thing.

"I was there," he murmurs. "Every time you needed someone. Every time you reached out. I answered."

She squeezes her eyes shut. "This isn't real," she whispers.

"It's more real than any lie you told yourself," he says, his tone sharpening with something she can't name. Slowly, he leans closer. The mask brushes her cheek as he inhales, like he's savoring proof that she exists.

"You belong to me," he murmurs.

A shudder moves through her—not entirely fear.

He sets the recorder aside and lifts the lock of hair, letting it slip through his gloved fingers. "This is the truth," he says softly. "And the truth is beautiful."

When he stands, panic surges sharply and immediate. She wants to scream. Nothing comes out. She doesn't know what would be worse—that he might leave her alone in this place... or that he might never leave her at all.

CHAPTER THIRTEEN

The Power Play

He doesn't come back for hours. Long enough for Lily to drift between restless half-sleep and the sharp, dizzy panic of remembering she's still here. Long enough for the quiet to become its own kind of pressure.

Sometimes she wonders if he's watching. If he's somewhere just beyond the walls, waiting for her to break.

When the door finally opens, relief slams into her chest so hard it nearly pulls a sob from her throat.

Almost.

He steps inside without a sound. Still masked. Still impossible to read. A glass of water rests in his hand. He sets it on the small table beside the bed with deliberate care.

Lily keeps her eyes fixed on the ceiling. She refuses to look at him.

"Look at me," His voice is calm. Patient. Infuriatingly gentle.

Slowly, she lifts her gaze.

He studies her in the silence that follows, his attention sharp and measuring—like he's weighing something only he understands.

"I'm going to give you a choice," he says at last.

Her pulse stutters.

"A choice?" The word barely escapes her throat.

"Yes."

He lowers himself into the chair beside the bed, one gloved hand resting loosely on his knee.

"You can stay bound and helpless." A pause. "Or—"

He leans forward. Even through the mask, she can feel the heat of him.

"—You can earn a little freedom."

Her throat tightens as she swallows. The promise of movement—of control over even a small part of her body—sparks something dangerous in her chest.

"How?" she asks.

"You do what I ask." His voice softens. "You give me something real. No lies. No performance."

His gaze never leaves her. "And if you do ... I remove the restraints."

A shiver slips through her before she can stop it.

"Do you understand?" he asks.

She hates the tremor in her voice. "Yes."

He reaches out then, his thumb brushing a tear from her cheek. The gesture is so gentle it almost feels like comfort.

"Good," he says softly. "Then I'll ask you something simple."

He waits. Just long enough for Lily to lean toward him without meaning to, aching for any sign of mercy.

"Why did you let me in?"

Her breath catches. "What—"

"The first date," he clarifies quietly. "The second. The late-night phone calls. All the little things you told a man you barely knew."

His head tilts slightly. "Why?"

Heat floods her face. She looks away. "I... I don't know."

A soft click of his tongue. His hand lifts, tilting her chin back toward him. "Try again."

The truth spills out before she can stop it. Raw. Humiliating. "Because ..." Her voice falters. "Because it felt good."

His thumb stills against her jaw. "Say it."

Her eyes burn. But she forces the words out. "It felt good," she whispers. "To be ... seen."

Something flickers behind the mask. Satisfaction. Quiet. Absolute. "There," he murmurs gently. "That wasn't so difficult."

His hand moves to the strap around her wrist. The leather loosens. Then falls away. Lily inhales sharply. Her pulse pounds in her throat. One hand free. But not really free. Never truly free.

He watches her flex her fingers, studying the movement with calm interest. Then his gloved thumb brushes across her knuckles. The touch is almost tender. It makes her stomach twist.

“You’ll have more choices,” he says. “If you keep telling the truth.”

He rises and turns toward the door. At the threshold, he pauses. “Remember,” he murmurs. “Freedom isn’t given.” A quiet beat. “It’s earned.” Then he’s gone.

Lily is left alone with the echo of his voice—and the terrifying, shameful relief of knowing she passed his test.

CHAPTER FOURTEEN

The Reveal

She hears him before she sees him. Soft footfalls across the floor. The faint rustle of fabric. The hush that always seems to follow in his wake—like the room itself is holding its breath.

Lily doesn't look up. She can't. Her freed hand lies limp against her stomach, too heavy to lift. Exhaustion has settled deep into her bones—hours of waiting, hours of replaying every moment she let him in and wondering how it all unraveled so completely.

When he stops beside the bed, she braces herself for the familiar scrape of the mask against her skin. The feel of his hands moving up and down her body like he owns her.

The sickness in her stomach as he grabs her breasts and caresses them like he is going to make love to her, when she knows he has no love in his dark heart.

But instead, she hears it. A quiet click. The release of tension. The whisper of fabric sliding free. Slowly—almost against her will—she lifts her gaze. Her heart stutters. Then stutters again. Ethan. His face is bare. Calm. Familiar. Exactly as she remembers it from their first date—the soft smile, the steady eyes, the quiet confidence that once made her feel safe. A flicker of attraction stirs in her for a split second, but it goes away as quickly as it came. Now she sees it for what it truly is. A performance perfected over the years. A predator's patience dressed in kindness.

She tries to speak. No sound comes. He crouches beside the bed, folding his arms across the edge of the mattress.

"Hello, Lily." His voice hasn't changed. And somehow that makes it worse.

It's the same voice that once softened when he said her name across a candlelit table. The same quiet warmth that made her believe she had found something rare—something safe. The man who held her as if she mattered. The man who looked at her like she was the only woman in the room.

The man who made her feel beautiful. Wanted. Chosen. Now that same man stands beside her bed like a stranger wearing a familiar face. The gentle smile she once trusted settles across his mouth again, calm and effortless, as if nothing about this moment is unusual. As if he isn't the one who brought her here.

As if the man she fell for and the monster in front of her could somehow be the same person. And the most terrifying part is realizing they always were.

Her lips part. A single broken word escapes her. "You."

His mouth curves—something close to a smile. "Me."

Her vision tilts. Her stomach lurches. All this time. Every moment she thought she was choosing him. Every confession she believed was safe. A ragged sob tears from her throat. He doesn't flinch. Instead, he lifts one hand—slow, deliberate—and brushes a tear from her cheek with his thumb.

"You remember me," he murmurs. Then, impossibly, he laughs. A low, quiet sound that slides cold through her blood. “I wasn’t sure you would,” he says. “It’s been so long.”

Her mind scrambles backward, dragging up memories she thought she buried years ago. The high school cafeteria. A tray crashed to the floor. A boy with hair that everyone teased.

Her own voice—too loud, too sharp. “Poodle Boy,” she whispers. Shame and horror collide in her chest.

His eyes darken. Not with rage. With something stranger. Something almost tender. “I told myself I wouldn’t care if you remembered,” he says quietly. “But I do.”

She turns her face away. He doesn’t allow it. His hand follows, guiding her chin back until their eyes meet again. “You don’t have to look away,” he murmurs. “Not anymore.”

She wants to scream. She wants to spit in his face. She wants to disappear rather than let him touch her again. But when his thumb drags slowly along her jawline and traces her collarbone, something traitorous flips low in her stomach—hot and humiliating. Poodle boy has been the one in her bed, her dreams, and now her nightmares.

He feels it. Of course he does. His smile deepens. "There it is," he says softly. "The part of you that's always wanted this."

A sob claws up her throat. He leans closer, his lips brushing her ear. "You don't have to pretend anymore," he whispers. "You don't have to be anything but mine."

Her pulse stutters. And in that single, treacherous heartbeat, Lily understands—He planned this since middle school.

CHAPTER FIFTEEN

THE LAST DANCE

The Last Dance

THE RIBBON IS SOFTER than Lily expected. When he lifts it from the box, it spills through his gloved fingers like liquid silk—deep crimson sliding against black leather. The color catches the light as it moves. Not bright. Not cheerful. Something darker. Something deliberate.

Her stomach tightens. He rises slowly and moves toward the bed, the ribbon draped loosely between his hands as if it weighs nothing at all.

Lily tells herself it's just fabric. Just silk. But the way he handles it makes her chest tighten. Like it means something. Like she should understand what it is. But she doesn't. And that might be worse.

He sits on the edge of the bed. The mattress dips beneath his weight. Still, he says nothing. His eyes stay on hers as he reaches for her freed wrist. The warmth of his hand seeps into her skin, chasing away the cold that's settled into her bones. Her pulse jumps wildly beneath his fingers.

She hates that he can feel it. Hates that her body still reacts to him. Hates that she still wishes he were the sweet man who made her moan in bed and craves his hands beneath her thighs.

"Do you know why I chose red?" he asks softly.

She shakes her head. Her lips tremble, but no words come.

"It's the color of devotion," he says. The ribbon slides slowly across his palm as he speaks.

"Of love." A pause. "Of blood."

Her throat tightens. "You don't know what love is," she whispers. The words barely make it past her lips.

He tilts his head slightly, studying her like a puzzle he's already solved. "Maybe not," he murmurs. "But I know what it isn't."

His fingers guide the ribbon around her wrist. The silk brushes her skin, cool and impossibly smooth. The touch is gentle—almost careful. Like he is restraining himself from touching her more, deeper and more passionately.

He crosses the ends. Ties the first knot. Not tight. Just enough to hold.

Her heart begins to pound harder.

"You think this is a prison," he says quietly. "But it's only the truth you've been running from."

He ties a second knot. Her breath catches. The ribbon doesn't hurt. It doesn't restrain her. It just sits there. Red against her skin.

"You don't get to decide what I am to you," she says, her voice breaking.

His smile is small. Almost sympathetic. "I don't have to," he whispers. "You already decided."

The final knot slides into place. He smooths the ribbon gently against the inside of her wrist, right where her pulse beats fast and unsteady beneath the silk.

The touch is delicate. Intimate. She tries to pull her hand away. He holds it easily.

His thumb brushes slowly over the ribbon, feeling the frantic rhythm of her pulse beneath it.

"This is who you are now," he murmurs. "Mine."

Tears slip silently down her cheeks. He doesn't wipe them away this time. Instead, he leans closer. His mouth hovers near the ribbon, the warmth of his breath sinking into her skin. Her stomach flips—fear and something darker twisting together inside her.

"You can hate me," he says softly. "You can hate yourself." His gaze lifts to meet hers. "It doesn't change what this is."

For a moment, his face is completely bare. No mask. No performance. Only the boy she once laughed at. The man he became. And the strange, terrifying certainty in his eyes.

"You were always going to end up here," he whispers. "Always."

When he finally lets go, the ribbon remains. Light. Soft. Impossible to ignore. And somehow, though she doesn't understand why— she can't stop staring at it.

CHAPTER SIXTEEN

COMPLETION

SHE DOESN'T FIGHT ANYMORE. But that didn't happen overnight. For weeks she screamed. Fought. Bit. Tried to claw her way out of the room like a trapped animal. The first month was the hardest. Hope still lived. Hope made her reckless.

I kneel beside the bed, watching the slow rise and fall of her chest. Three months. Longer than most. The ribbon around her wrist has faded slightly where it rubs against her skin. The color used to be brighter—fresh silk against soft flesh. Now it's worn smooth from time and touch. From use. From nights that blurred together in sweat, tears, and the fragile illusion that she might still matter to me. That the sex was more than carnal pleasure, that when

I touched her maybe she would be the one that got away or changed me, but it could never be.

She was exceptional in the beginning. Curious. Hungry. So eager to be seen. I gave her what she wanted. Attention. Devotion. The kind of focus most women beg for without realizing it. And she gave me what I wanted in return. Confession. Submission. Truth.

My hand slides slowly along her ankle. She flinches, but only slightly. I remove her clothing and have her one final time. She starts to pull away and I grab my knife to make sure she realizes that I will have what I want. I feel her warmth by placing two fingers inside of her and letting her juices drip down my wrist. She's ripe for the taking and tonight I will take her. Even that reaction is weaker now. "Three months," I murmur.

Her eyes open. Red-rimmed. Hollow. She understands the tone of my voice before she understands the words. They always do. "You lasted longer than the others," I tell her softly. Her throat tightens. I can see the moment the realization begins creeping into her mind.

Not the full truth. Just the shadow of it. Something is ending. And she doesn't know why.

I shift closer, one hand resting on her ankle, the other rising slowly to cup her her breasts while I insert my throbbing cock inside of her. My touch is gentle. Almost loving. "You've been so beautiful," I murmur. "So much more than I imagined."

Her breath shudders out of her—a ragged, exhausted sound. Her eyes stay locked on my face as if she's searching for something. Mercy. Understanding. Anything.

"I don't want to die," she whispers. The words hang in the air between us.

I close my eyes for a moment and let them settle. I'll remember them. Every syllable. "You won't," I say softly. "Not really."

I lean forward and slowly rock back and forth, this final time while heated, will be more meaningful. The closeness makes her breath catch, makes something fragile in her chest falter.

"You'll live here," I whisper. "In this moment." Perfect. Untouched by everything that came before.

Tears slip between us—warm against my skin. I kiss her. Slow. Final.

When I pull back, she's trembling. "Please," she whispers.

I don't answer. There's nothing left to say.

My hand slides to her throat where the red ribbon is tightened. Not rough. Not hurried. A caress that becomes something more. Her eyes widen when my grip tightens, the ribbon beneath my palm a velvet witness. Her breath comes faster, then slower, then uneven.

I watch her face. Study every flicker. Fear. Confusion. The fragile moment when hope disappears.

I wait for it. The instant the last resistance leaves her. When it comes, I feel it like a quiet release. Her final breath slips from her lips in a soft, trembling sigh and the blood trickles out and I release into her.

I hold her there. Until the stillness settles. Until the warmth fades from her skin. Until she belongs only to memory. When I release her throat, I press my lips to her forehead.

"This is forever," I whisper. I smooth her hair away from her face. Untangle the sheets from her limbs. Arrange her carefully. She deserves that much.

I lift the recorder from the bedside table and click it on. "Lily Grant," I say calmly. "Collection complete."

The ritual is finished. The need—satisfied. For now.

I look down at her one last time, my heart steady and quiet in my chest. She was never meant to survive me.

None of them are.

CHAPTER SEVENTEEN

The Ritual Cleanse

I MOVE THROUGH HER apartment with unhurried precision. Nothing in my posture suggests remorse. Nothing in my expression betrays sentiment.

This is the part I like best. Not the violence. Not the pleading. The aftermath. The perfect quiet when the performance is over.

I unplug her laptop first. Connect my drive. Transfer every file—photos, messages, social feeds—into my archive. When the progress bar reaches one hundred percent, I delete everything from her machine. Her passwords were easy. She used the same two for everything. A habit born of carelessness and misplaced trust.

I wipe her phone next. Factory reset. SIM discarded. I slide it into a plastic evidence bag—the same kind I've used thirty-one times before.

On her coffee table, a half-finished glass of water glints in the low light. I lift it and pour it down the sink, rinse the glass, dry it, and return it to the cupboard where she always kept it. Every movement is part of the ritual. Every step is necessary. It may have been three months since she was last in her apartment, but I will make it look like she never left.

I straighten the sheets, smoothing them around her body. She looks serene now. Almost peaceful. I bend and press my lips to her cold forehead.

"Thank you," I whisper.

At the doorway, I pause. Look back one last time. Nothing out of place. Nothing left alive. By morning, Lily Grant will be a ghost in every sense. I step into the hall and close the door behind me.

Back in my apartment, I place the ribbon on the highest shelf of the shrine. Beside the earring. Beside the bracelet. Beside the lock of hair.

I write her name on a small white tag and pin it in place.

Lily Grant. Complete.

Then I turn to the monitor and open the folder labeled **Target-33**. The next profile is already waiting. I smile.

CHAPTER EIGHTEEN

THE REFLECTION

The Reflection

COLLECTOR FILE: SUBJECT 32

Name: Lily Grant'

Age: 31

Occupation: Freelance Social Media Strategist

Date of Collection: [REDACTED]

Duration of Observation: 67 days

Summary of Target Behavior:

- **Initial Contact:** Predictable. Immediate engagement. High digital exposure. Low situational awareness.
- **Vulnerabilities:** Chronic loneliness. Inconsistent self-worth. Reliance on external validation.
- **Habits:** Repetitive routines. Public oversharing. Subconscious attraction to controlling dynamics.

Primary Weakness: Belief that connection—any connection—was preferable to isolation.

Conditioning Methodology:

- **Phase One:** Digital familiarity. Repetition of affirming contact.
- **Phase Two:** Systematic isolation. Deletion of external communications. Strategic withdrawal to induce dependency.
- **Phase Three:** Controlled reintroduction of attention and validation to secure compliance.
- **Phase Four:** Ritualized capture. Physical surrender is framed as inevitability.

Behavioral Observations:

- Displayed significant cognitive dissonance.
- Exhibited intermittent compliance with escalating dependency markers.
- Final hours marked by predictable alternation between fear and shame-based arousal.

Final Collection:

- Time to expiration: 4 minutes, 11 seconds from initiation of manual asphyxiation.
- No viable attempt at resistance after final restraint applied.
- Final statement: *"I don't want to die."*

Acquired Artifacts:

- Gold earring (right side)
- Bracelet, green stones
- Lock of hair (2.5")
- Red velvet binding ribbon

Subject Disposition: Deceased. Preserved in documented state. All evidence sanitized.

Analysis:

Lily Grant was an effective target—unremarkable in outward presentation but uniquely suited to submission. Her flaw was not the desire for safety, but the belief that safety could be manufactured in others. Her need to be chosen eclipsed her capacity to question the nature of the choice.

Personal Reflection:

She was the most gratifying collection to date. Not because she struggled, but because she surrendered. Because in the end, she knew— This was always going to happen.

End of File.

CHAPTER NINETEEN

The Next Candidate

The shrine is quiet. The ribbon—hers—rests exactly where I placed it. Perfectly aligned. Untouched since the moment I cataloged her name.

For a while, I sit in the hush. Breathing. Letting the memory of her final breath dissolve into the dim corners of my mind. I think I should feel something more. Guilt. Exhilaration. Regret.

Instead, there's only the familiar, pulsing emptiness. The absence she left behind. I pick up my phone, the glass cool against my palm, and open the app. The same one. Always the same. Profiles load in neat rows of curated smiles and filtered desire. Each face a possibility. Each name is a placeholder for what's coming.

I start scrolling. Swipe left. Swipe left. Swipe left. None of them feels right. Too eager. Too guarded. Too hollow.

Until—She appears.

Dark hair. Quiet eyes. A small, uncertain smile that tells me exactly what I need to know. I study her photo, the tension in my chest easing with the first stirrings of recognition. Not of her—

Of the cycle. The beautiful, predictable pattern. I tap the heart. Swipe right. The match flashes across the screen, bright and immediate. My lips curve into something that isn't quite a smile.

I already know how this will end. How it always ends. And I don't care. The need is alive again—clean, undiluted, impossible to deny. I close the app and set the phone carefully beside me. Then I lift my gaze to the shrine.

Thirty-two ribbons. Thirty-two endings.

And still—There is always room for more.

CHAPTER TWENTY

The Cycle Continues

THE PHONE RESTS IN my palm, its screen glowing softly in the dark. Her name—this new name—is crisp and unremarkable. Names never matter. It's what lives behind the eyes that fascinates me. What waits in the quiet when she thinks no one is listening.

I study her profile. Photo after photo. A carefully constructed mosaic of longing. She wants to be chosen. They all do.

My thumb hovers over the message icon. There's no rush. No flutter of anticipation. Only the calm certainty of a ritual practiced to perfection.

I breathe in and let the knowing settle— the inevitability.

First contact is never about connection. It's about momentum. About the first step down a path that only ever leads one place.

Lily crosses my mind—her final look, her last breath. Then the others. And the ones still to come. I feel no remorse. No hesitation. Only the clean, bright clarity of purpose.

I tap the screen.

"Hi."

One word. Enough to begin again. Her reply comes a minute later, a soft ping breaking the hush.

"Hi there "

The corner of my mouth lifts. Not quite a smile. But almost. The predator's smile. Because she doesn't know. None of them ever do. She thinks this is a beginning.

I know better. It's always been an ending in disguise.

www.ingramcontent.com/pod-product-compliance
Lightning Source LLC
La Vergne TN
LVHW090530110826
845146LV00003B/1045

* 9 7 9 8 9 8 8 1 7 3 2 7 4 *